The CATS on Ben YeHuda Street

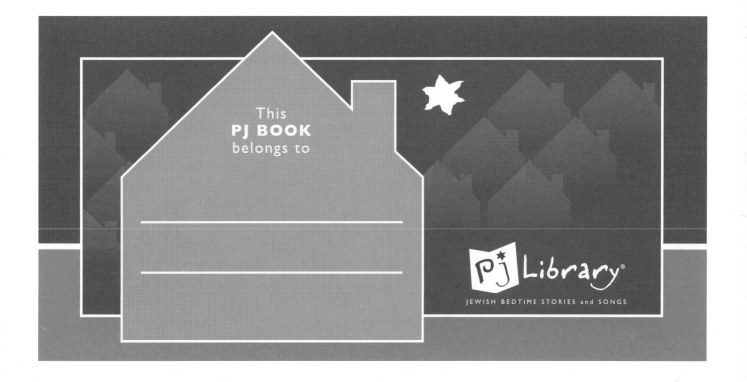

This **PJ BOOK** belongs to

_____

_____

PJ Library®

JEWISH BEDTIME STORIES and SONGS

In memory of Sandy Roberts—A.R.C.

To my mother and my father,
my brightest stars—F.C.

Text copyright © 2013 by Ann Redisch Stampler
Illustrations copyright © 2013 by Francesca Carabelli

Kar-Ben Publishing
A division of Lerner Publishing Group, Inc.
241 First Avenue North
Minneapolis, MN 55401 U.S.A.

Website address: www.karben.com

Library of Congress Cataloging-in-Publication Data

Stampler, Ann Redisch.
    The cats on Ben Yehuda Street / by Ann Redisch Stampler : illustrated by
Francesca Carabelli.
        p.   cm.
    Summary: Mrs. Spiegel loves her two cats while her grumpy neighbor,
Mr. Modiano, claims they are useless but when Ketzie goes missing, it is Mr.
Modiano who searches the streets of Tel Aviv all night to find her.
    ISBN 978–0–7613–8123–5 (lib. bdg. : alk. paper)
    [1. Cats—Fiction. 2. Neighbors—Fiction. 3. Tel Aviv (Israel)—Fiction. 4. Israel—
Fiction.] I. Carabelli, Francesca, ill. II. Title.
PZ7.S78614Cat 2013
[E]—dc23   2012009503

PJ Library Edition ISBN 978-0-7613-8125-9

Manufactured in Hong Kong
3-45203-12334-12/14/2017

061827.9K3/B0866/A6

The Cats on Ben Yehuda Street

By Ann Redisch Stampler

Illustrated by Francesca Carabelli

KAR-BEN
PUBLISHING

Up and down Ben Yehuda Street: cats, cats, cats. Cats curling up on benches and stretching underneath. Cats licking their paws on porches and climbing in leafy branches.

Free cats, fat cats, living-on-the-sidewalk cats. Cats with no collars—for collars show that cats belong to somebody, and street cats belong to no one but themselves.

"Messy, meowing, useless cats!" muttered Mr. Modiano as he unlocked the Tel Aviv Fish Palace each morning. All day long, he shooed cats from his doorway.

But every night, when Mr. Modiano climbed the stairs to his apartment, two cats dozed on a cushion by Mrs. Spiegel's door.

"Your cat brings more cats!" He pointed at Ketzie, Mrs. Spiegel's little grey cat with a pink collar lying on a pillow next to Gatito, a fluffy white cat with no collar at all.

Then Mr. Modiano would give Mrs. Spiegel whatever fish he had left over, arranged on a platter just so. "This fish is fit for a queen, not for cats," he warned.

"Thank you," Mrs. Spiegel said, "and would you maybe like to come in for a little tea?"

But Mr. Modiano always said no: *"Lo, lo, lo."*

As soon as Mr. Modiano closed his door, Mrs. Spiegel put the fish into a bowl for the two cats to share.

But the apartment building rule said, "Just One Cat," so after dinner, only Ketzie could come inside.

Mrs. Spiegel liked the way
Ketzie helped her knit,

and the way Ketzie kept her
company in the kitchen.

She liked it when Ketzie licked her face to wake her up in the morning.

She liked the way Ketzie was always there.

One night Mr. Modiano brought salmon. "This is for *you*, not for your cat!" he said, just barely stroking Gatito's back.

"Thank you," Mrs. Spiegel said. "Would you like to maybe come in for a little tea?"

Mr. Modiano always said no: *"lo, lo, lo."*

The next night, Mr. Modiano brought a plate of pickled herring. "I almost tripped on this wild animal!" he muttered, just barely tickling Gatito's tail.

"A nice cat like this would keep you company," Mrs. Spiegel told him.

"Company!" Mr. Modiano frowned. "What does an old man need with messy, meowing company?"

"Well, would you like to maybe come in for a little tea?" she asked.

Mr. Modiano always said no:
"lo, lo, lo."

Every morning Mrs. Spiegel walked to the beach with Ketzie to breathe in the salty smell of the Mediterranean Sea.

As soon as they neared the waves, Ketzie ran home. She didn't like to be so close to the water.

When Ketzie got home from the beach, she and Gatito waited on the porch for Mrs. Spiegel to return . . . until one day, when Ketzie wasn't there!

"Where is Ketzie?" asked Mrs. Spiegel.

Gatito's nose was poking through the railing as if he was looking for Ketzie too.

Mrs. Spiegel clomped downstairs. She searched up and down Ben Yehuda Street, between the buildings, and under the tables at the sidewalk cafe. She asked everyone she met, "Have you seen my Ketzie?"

Everybody had seen plump cats and skinny cats, spotted cats and striped cats, but no little grey cat with a pink collar.

Everybody pointed to wrong-sized, wrong-colored, wrong-faced cats.

Mrs. Spiegel dragged her sad self home. Mr. Modiano was leaning out the door of the Fish Palace, shooing away cats. "What's wrong, silly Gatito?" he said.

"He isn't silly!" Mrs. Spiegel said. "Ketzie is gone!"

"Cats!" said Mr. Modiano. "Maybe she ran away."

Mrs. Spiegel burst into tears and clomped up to her apartment.

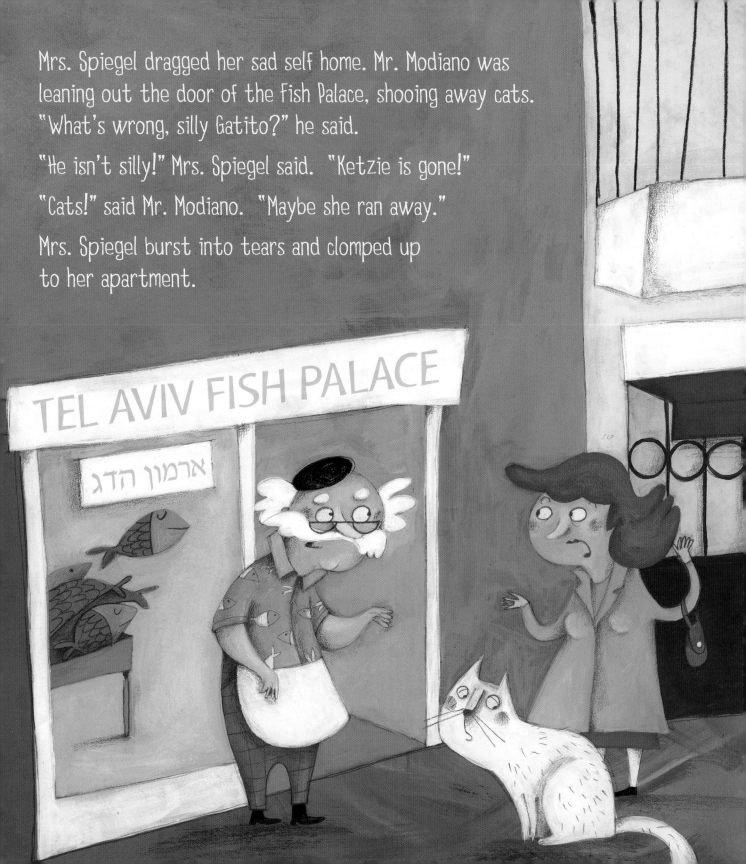

TEL AVIV FISH PALACE

ארמון הדג

She tried to eat, but she wasn't hungry. She tried to knit, but without Ketzie in her lap, she couldn't. When Mr. Modiano came by, she did not invite him in for tea.

"I know you have a low opinion of cats," she said. "But my Ketzie would never run away. If not for something terrible happening, my Ketzie would come back."

Mr. Modiano left quietly. Then a most unusual thing happened. Mrs. Spiegel heard the noisy putt-putting of a motor scooter in the alley. There sat Mr. Modiano, perched on the back of his scooter. "Don't worry!" he called up to Mrs. Spiegel.

"Hmmff!" Mrs. Spiegel muttered. As if she would worry about a cat-hating man like Mr. Modiano!

Mrs. Spiegel paced up and down in her apartment. She thought about going to bed, but the idea of waking up without Ketzie there to lick her face made her cry.

Then, long after midnight, she heard putt-putting in the alley. Outside on the porch, Gatito meowed, and then there was more meowing!

Mrs. Spiegel ran down the stairs. Mr. Modiano held
a little grey cat with a pink collar, her front leg
sticking straight out in a stiff, white cast.

"My Ketzie!" Mrs. Spiegel cried, burying her face in
the soft, grey fur.

"Cats!" said Mr. Modiano, gently cradling Ketzie, as Gatito rubbed against his leg. "I found her at the animal hospital. She must have had a tussle with a car—silly cat! But she's going to be fine."

The next morning, Mrs. Spiegel put Ketzie in a basket to walk to the sea. "We'll just get close enough to smell the salt," she said.

But when they got back, Gatito was not on the landing! Not only that, the cushion was gone, too!

5

"Oh no!" said Mrs. Spiegel.

Just then, Mr. Modiano opened his door.

Sitting neatly on the cushion in the middle of the living room,
just so, was a fluffy white cat with a new blue collar: Gatito!

"Don't look so surprised," said Mr. Modiano. "You think I want to hunt all night for this one, too?"

Mrs. Spiegel smiled. "Mr. Modiano," she said. "Would you like to maybe come in for a little tea?"

Mr. Modiano said, *"Lo, lo, lo."*

Then he opened his door even wider and he smiled, too.
"But maybe I could make a cup of tea for *you*," he said. "And
a saucer of milk for your cat . . . "

About the Author and Illustrator

Ann Redisch Stampler is the author of both picture books and young adult fiction. Her picture books include National Jewish Book Award winner *The Rooster Prince of Breslov*, as well as *The Wooden Sword; Go Home, Mrs. Beekman!; Shlemazel and the Remarkable Spoon of Pohost;* and *Something for Nothing*. She's also the author of a young adult novel, *Where It Began*. The Eastern European folktales that started her picture book career were beloved stories she heard from her immigrant grandmother. Born on the East Coast and raised mostly in the West, she lives in Los Angeles.

Francesca Carabelli lives and works in Rome, Italy. An illustrator of several books for major international publishers, her mother says she was born with a drawing pencil in her hand.